Ghost GoaLie

GHOST GOALIE

J. BURCHETT AND S. VOGLER

ILLUSTRATED by Guy Parker-Rees

BLOOMSBURY

LONDON BERLIN NEW YORK

Bloomsbury Publishing, London, Berlin and New York

First published in Great Britain in 1998 by Bloomsbury Publishing Plc
36 Soho Square, London, W1D 3QY
This edition published in July 2010

A CIP catalogue record of this book is available from the British Library

ISBN 978 1 4088 0826 9

FSC
Mixed Sources
Product group from well-managed
forests and other controlled sources
Cert no. SGS-COC-2061
www.fsc.org
© 1996 Forest Stewardship Council

Printed in Great Britain by Clays Ltd, St Ives plc, Bungay, Suffolk

1 3 5 7 9 10 8 6 4 2

www.bloomsbury.com/childrens

Ghost Goalie

Nervous smiles

Knocking knees

bitten fingernails

Nervous fidget

Billy Bright and the Tigers had an important football match to play on Saturday. It was their most important match ever. Only two teams were left in the knock-out competition – the Tigers and Rockfield Rangers.

The winners would get tickets to see the FA Cup Final.

Everyone in the team was excited. Everyone had trained hard. Everyone was fit. Everyone except their coach – Billy's dad.

Billy's dad was at home. He was covered in spots. He had

his hands in mittens to stop him scratching. Billy's dad had chickenpox. Mum said he wasn't allowed out.

It was two days before the match. The Tigers were practising in Tottingham Town park. They were having trouble.

Billy sat on the pitch. He put
his head in his hands. The
Tigers were a skilful side but
they were lost without Dad.
With Dad's coaching they had
won their last match four-nil.
They had played brilliantly.
But now look at them!

'What are we going to do?'
groaned Billy. The Tigers
Under-Tens Football Club
didn't stand a chance on
Saturday. They were in big
trouble.

'You're in big trouble,' said a
voice. Billy got up. A man was

standing in front of him. Billy thought he must be in fancy dress. And he knew he'd seen him somewhere before.

The man seemed a bit wobbly round the edges. Billy rubbed his eyes. He looked again. The man *was* wobbly round the edges! And Billy could see right through him! It was like looking through a lemon jelly. The man was . . . a ghost!

'Hello, Billy,' said the ghost.

'How do you know my name?' gasped Billy.

'I've been watching the Tigers,' said the ghost. 'You're a good side. But you're lost

without your coach. Where's
Dad?'

'Chickenpox,' muttered Billy.
'. . . silly illness for a grown-
up.'

'Oh dear,' said the ghost.
'Tell him not to scratch.'

The Tigers were mooching off
the pitch.

'We'll never find another
coach before Saturday,' sighed
Billy.

'Yes you will,' said the ghost.

'How?' asked Billy.

'I'll be your coach,' said
the ghost. 'Let me just check
my Phantom In Football
Association Rules . . .

15

. . . Yes, no problem. Rule twenty-five. If the official coach can't be there – that's your dad – a ghost substitute can be used – that's me. It'll be great to be with a Tottingham Town team again. Springer will be back in the game at last. Right, let's get started.'

'Springer?' said Billy. 'I know who you are. You're the great Springer Spannell!'

'That's me,' said Springer. Springer rolled his ball along one arm, across his shoulders and down to the other hand. Billy gawped. That was skill.

'My dad's got your photo,' said Billy. 'He says you were

the best goalkeeper ever. You
saved that penalty for
Tottingham Town FC in the
Cup Final. Tottingham Town
were never the same after you
retired.'

Springer spun his ball on his
finger, flicked it in the air and
punched it to Billy. Billy tried

to head it. The ball went
straight through him.

'Let's sort this team out,' said
Springer. 'You want to win
those tickets, don't you?'

Billy couldn't believe it. The
Tigers were going to get help –
from a professional footballer!

And not just any professional. Springer Spannell himself – the goalie whose last minute save had won the cup for Tottingham Town. People still talked about it.

'Listen everyone,' yelled Billy. 'It's going to be all right. I've found us a coach. A professional footballer. He's going to help us win on Saturday.'

'When's he coming?' asked Blocker.

'He's here,' said Billy.

'Where?' demanded Rob.

'There!' Billy pointed at Springer.

'What are you talking about?' said Bullseye.

'That's the goalpost, Billy,' said Mona.

Springer began to dribble his ball round the team. They took no notice. Billy finally realised they couldn't see the ghost!

'Get yourself out of that,' chuckled Springer. 'I'm only allowed to appear to one person.' He pulled out the rule book.

'Rule seven,' he read. 'A ghost coach – that's me – can only appear to one member of the team – that's you. And if anyone else finds out, the coach gets the sack – I disappear.'

'Why didn't you say so before?' said Billy crossly.

'Say what?' asked Terry.

'You feeling all right?' said Ellen.

'I think he's got chickenpox in his brain,' laughed Joe.

'Tell them *you'll* be their coach,' said Springer.

'I'll be your coach,' said Billy.

'You're not a professional,' said Rick.

'Pretend you've got a book,' said Springer.

'I've got a book,' said Billy.

'What's that got to do with football?' asked Lisa.

'It's a coaching book,' said Springer.

'It's a coaching book,' said Billy.

'But you're not a coach,' said Kim. 'And it's only two days to the final.' The team looked fed up.

'Tell them you're going to win,' said Springer.

'We're going to win,' said Billy. 'The Tigers are going to Wembley!'

'How did the practice go?'
asked Dad at teatime. Dad was
trying to eat his fish and chips
with his mittens on.

'It wasn't good,' said Billy.
'But I've got help . . .' Dad
wasn't listening. 'How was
Rick's footwork?'

'Not great,' said Billy. 'He had a pile up with Terry and Lisa and Bullseye. But . . .'

'What about Rob's throw-ins?' asked Dad.

'Not perfect,' said Billy. 'He was too busy arguing. But . . .'

'Did Blocker get his sliding tackle right?' asked Dad.

'His shorts fell down,' said Billy. 'We gave up then.'

'Look Billy,' said Dad.

Dodgy elastic →

'You're only kids. You need a grown-up to coach you . . . We'd better pull out of the final.'

Billy's mouth dropped open.

'No, Dad,' he said. 'It's okay. I've got . . .'

'I know it's disappointing,' said Dad. 'But it's for the best.'

'I'm trying to tell you!' shouted Billy, almost in tears. 'I've got help.'

'Who?' asked Dad.

'A proper footballer . . .' Billy stopped. He'd forgotten! He mustn't say anything about Springer.

'. . . I mean . . . I've got a proper footballer's book. *I'll* do the training.'

'But you're not a coach, Billy,' said Dad. 'You're only nine.'

'Give me a chance,' said Billy. 'Just one chance. Please!'

'Well,' said Dad. 'You can practise tomorrow but I don't think . . .'

'Great!' said Billy. He'd show Dad the Tigers could do it.

On Friday morning, Billy raced to the park. The team were all there. They still looked fed up. And there was no sign of Springer. Had Billy really met him yesterday? Or had he just imagined it?

'Go on then, Billy,' said Ellen. 'What do we do?'

'Um . . .' said Billy.
'Springer!' he whispered.

'Spring-up?' said Joe. 'What's a spring-up?'

'And where's your book?' asked Rob.

'Er . . .' said Billy. 'It's at home.'

Billy had to think fast. He hadn't got a book.

'Aren't we going to warm up?' asked Mona.

'Erm . . .' said Billy. 'Yes. Twenty laps of the pitch.' That should give Springer a chance to turn up.

31

'Twenty!' shrieked Blocker.
'Your dad always says two.'
'It's in the book,' said Billy.
The team set off, groaning.
Billy was so busy looking
round for Springer that he

bumped into Blocker, tripped
Terry up, and ran into the
goalpost.

'Steady on,' said a voice. It
was Springer.

'Where've you been?' panted
Billy. 'I've been waiting for
you.'

'I'm going as fast as I can,'
gasped Rob, as he ran past.

'Not you, Rob,' sighed Billy.
'I was talking to the ghos . . .
goalpost.' Rob gave him a
funny look. The whole team
were giving him funny looks.

'I thought you weren't
coming,' Billy whispered to
Springer. 'Sorry, lad,' said
Springer. 'The town hall clock
must be slow.'

The Tigers collapsed at Billy's feet. They'd had enough.

'What do we do now?' Billy asked Springer.

'Why are you asking us?' said Rick.

'You're the one with the book,' moaned Ellen.

'I'm off,' said Blocker.

'Quick!' said Springer. 'Get them on the pitch.'

'Tapping and passing,' shouted Springer, as soon as the Tigers were ready. He tapped his ball to Billy. Billy went to boot it back. His foot

passed straight through the ghost ball. He fell over.

'What are you doing?' asked Kim.

'Er . . . body feint,' said Billy. 'It's in the book.'

Springer was very excited to be back on the pitch. He dribbled his football here. He volleyed it there. He dived about in the goalmouth. He kept forgetting he was supposed to be a coach. Billy coughed to get his attention.

'Got a cold, Billy?' asked Kim. Billy waved his arms.

'Is that a new signal?' said Bullseye. In the end, Billy had to go and fetch Springer from the goal.

'Sorry, lad,' said Springer. 'I forgot. But it's great to be back in the game.'

So Springer coached Billy and Billy coached the Tigers. By the end of the practice, the Tigers were fast, they were accurate and they were playing like a team again. They'd even got used to Billy talking to himself, swinging his foot at nothing and shouting 'Springer!' into thin air.

'It's in the book,' Billy said.

When Billy got home, Dad was doing the ironing in his mittens.

'It was brilliant today, Dad,' said Billy. 'No loose passes, good clean tackles and you should have seen it when . . .'

Ding-dong! went the doorbell.

Springer was standing on the doorstep.

'I've come for our pre-match tactics talk,' he said.

'Great,' whispered Billy. 'Come in.'

'Who is it?' asked Dad.

'Er . . . wrong house,' called Billy. Springer dribbled his ball down the hall and into the lounge. He did some sit-ups on the carpet. Dad just carried on ironing.

'Now, Billy,' said Dad.

'About the final tomorrow . . .'

'It's going to be great. We were really on form today. You should have seen it when Rob passed to me and I swerved round Terry and I wrong-footed Ellen and I blasted it at

goal.' He winked at Springer.
'No one could have saved it.'

'Come on, Billy,' said Dad. 'I
know you're dying to play in
the final but it's just not on.
Kids coaching kids. Whoever
heard of it?'

Springer looked horrified.

'He's going to pull you out of
the final!' he said.

'I'm going to pull you out of
the final,' said Dad.

'But you can't!' wailed Billy.
'The practice really was good.
Ask anyone.' Dad shook his
head. Springer started pacing
up and down.

'I bet no one tried to stop
Tottingham Town play in that

Cup Final,' said Billy.
'Everybody said they were no-hopers but they won.'

'True,' said Dad. 'But . . .'

'What would Springer Spannell say if he was here now?' said Billy.

'I'd say go for it,' said Springer.

He'd say go for it

'He'd say go for it,' said
Billy.

Dad looked at his picture
of Springer Spannell of
Tottingham Town FC.

'Okay,' he said. 'You win.'

'We will,' said Billy and
Springer.

It was Saturday. It was the
final. Billy and the Tigers and
Springer ran out on to the town
pitch. Their supporters cheered.
Dad waved his mittens from the
back of the car. It was going to
be a tough game. Rockfield
Rangers were a good side.

The Tigers huddled round for
their pre-match talk.

'Now remember what I said

last night,' Springer told Billy.

'Lisa, watch out for that big striker,' said Billy. 'Terry, their winger has a mean left foot and Blocker . . .'

'Don't worry, Coach,' whispered Blocker. 'My mum's

put extra strong elastic in my shorts.'

'Good,' said Billy. 'Now Tigers, mark tight, look for that loose ball and play like a team.'

'Couldn't have put it better myself,' said Springer.

Rockfield Rangers won the toss. The referee blew his whistle. The final had started. The Rangers kicked off. They took the ball down the left wing. With a brilliant one-two the strikers wrong-footed the Tigers' defence. Billy waited for Springer to shout instructions. He didn't. Billy looked over to the touchline. Springer wasn't there!

Billy tried to keep his eyes on the game but where was Springer? The Rangers' striker found the gap and volleyed the ball at the goal. Mona missed it. And there was Springer – doing a fantastic save! Well, it

would have been a fantastic
save if he hadn't been a ghost.
The ball sailed straight through
his hands. The Tigers were
one-nil down.

'Springer, what are you
doing?' yelled Billy. 'Get back
to the touchline!'

'Back to the touchline?' said

Blocker. 'But I've only just come on.'

'Not you, Blocker,' sighed Billy.

Springer bounded over.

'Sorry, lad,' he said. 'But it would have been a brilliant save.'

'You're our coach,' hissed Billy. 'We need you on the touchline . . . Perhaps we'd be better off without you,' he muttered.

'I did my best,' wailed Mona.

'Not you, Mona,' sighed Billy.

'You've got to go to the touchline,' Billy whispered to Springer. 'Check your rules.'

'I could help in midfield?'

'Check your rules!'

Springer looked at his book.

'Rule thirty-five,' he sighed. 'The ghost coach – that's me – has to stay on the touchline – that's over there.'

'Billy!' shouted Bullseye. 'We're kicking off.'

It was the hardest game the Tigers had ever played. Twenty minutes into the second half they were still one-nil down. And if Springer hadn't been coaching it would have been more. The team began to give up. They couldn't break

through the Rangers' defensive
wall. Billy finally got
possession. But it was hardly
worth trying. The Rangers'
defence were on their way.
Then suddenly,

'Bullseye's unmarked!' yelled
Springer. Billy looked up. There

was Bullseye making a run on his left. Billy lobbed a perfect pass to his feet.

'Good work,' shouted Springer. Bullseye hammered the ball at the goal. It hit the post! The crowd gasped. He ran in for another shot. As the

goalie came out, Bullseye
chipped the ball over his head.
The Tigers had equalised!

Now they played like a team
that could win. It was the
Rangers' turn to look worried.

'We can make it,' thought
Billy. And that was when he

made his mistake. Ellen had the
ball. She was about to kick it
up the field. She didn't notice
the Rangers' striker sprinting
up to her.

'Striker onside!' screamed Springer. 'Clear the ball!' And Billy forgot that Ellen couldn't hear Springer. He didn't warn her. He just gaped as the Rangers' striker slipped in and hammered the ball towards the net.

But Mona saved the game. With a tremendous leap she punched the ball over the bar. It was a save that Springer himself would have been proud of. Springer danced on the touchline.

But time was running out. The referee kept checking his watch. It was going to be a draw. The Rangers had the ball. And

then, with a brilliant sliding
tackle, Blocker won possession.

Rick pounced on the ball and
tapped it to Kim.

Kim flicked it straight on to
Rob.

Rob passed to Bullseye.

And Billy saw his chance.
He found a space.
'Bullseye!' he yelled. He
controlled the pass and got
ready to shoot at goal. But the
referee was putting the whistle
to his mouth.

'To his right!' shouted
Springer.

And, as the Rangers' goalie
dived to his left, Billy blasted
the ball into the back of the

net. The whistle blew. The crowd went wild. Springer did a somersault. The Tigers had won. They were going to Wembley.

The Tigers hugged each other. They waved to Billy's dad. They hugged Billy. Billy shook hands with the air.

The team looked at him.

'It's in the book,' said Billy.